Bus

Please renew/return items by last date shown. Please call the number below:

Renewals and enquiries:   0300 1234049

Textphone for hearing or speech impaired users:   01992 555506

www.hertfordshire.gov.uk/libraries

L32

Hertfordshire

First published 2022 by Walker Books Ltd
87 Vauxhall Walk, London SE11 5HJ

2 4 6 8 10 9 7 5 3 1

Printed in China

British Library Cataloguing in Publication Data:
a catalogue record for this book is
available from the British Library.

ISBN 978-1-5295-0736-2

www.walker.co.uk

# Maisy's Snowy Day

## Lucy Cousins

WALKER BOOKS
AND SUBSIDIARIES
LONDON • BOSTON • SYDNEY • AUCKLAND

One day, Maisy wakes up to a wonderful surprise. It's snowing!

After breakfast, she gets ready and puts on her coat and hat, her scarf, gloves, warm woolly socks and boots.

Brrr, it's very cold outside!

The snow on the ground
is soft and scrunchy.

Maisy puts seeds out for
the hungry birds to eat.

Scrunch
Scrunch
Scrunch

It's time for Maisy to go to the park and meet her friends.

Her boots leave footprints in the snow as she walks along.

Eddie and Cyril are trying to
catch snowflakes
as they fall.

Maisy and Tallulah roll the snow into big balls.

Cyril and Eddie put the snowballs on top of each other.

Charley finds twigs
for whiskers and
pebbles for a nose,
eyes and mouth.

It's a snow Maisy!

Eddie blows snow with his trunk as they climb up a big hill.

It's time
for a sledge race.
Ready, steady... GO!

Watch out for the bumps!

Oh dear, now Cyril is cold. Maisy gives him a cuddle to warm him up.

The sun is setting and it's getting dark in the park. Time to go home.

Maisy's house is covered in twinkly lights that shine brightly in the dark. It looks so pretty! Maisy invites everyone inside.

All the friends are cosy and happy together. Maisy makes hot chocolate, the perfect treat to end a lovely, snowy day!